A Note to Parents and Caregivers:

Read-it! Readers are for children who are just starting on the amazing road to reading. These beautiful books support both the acquisition of reading skills and the love of books.

The RED LEVEL presents familiar topics using common words and repeating sentence patterns.

The BLUE LEVEL presents new ideas using a larger vocabulary and varied sentence structure.

The YELLOW LEVEL presents more challenging ideas, a broad vocabulary, and wide variety in sentence structure.

The GREEN LEVEL presents more complex ideas, an extended vocabulary range, and expanded language structures.

When sharing a book with your child, read in short stretches, pausing often to talk about the pictures. Have your child turn the pages and point to the pictures and familiar words. And be sure to reread favorite stories or parts of stories.

There is no right or wrong way to share books with children. Find time to read with your child, and pass on the legacy of literacy.

Adria F. Klein, Ph.D.
Professor Emeritus
California State University
San Bernardino, California

Managing Editor: Bob Temple
Creative Director: Terri Foley
Editor: Brenda Haugen
Editorial Adviser: Andrea Cascardi
Copy Editor: Laurie Kahn
Designer: Melissa Voda
Page production: The Design Lab
The illustrations in this book were prepared digitally.

Picture Window Books
5115 Excelsior Boulevard
Suite 232
Minneapolis, MN 55416
1-877-845-8392
www.picturewindowbooks.com

Printed in the United States of America.

Library of Congress Cataloging-in-Publication Data
Blair, Eric.
Snow White / by Jacob and Wilhelm Grimm ; adapted by Eric Blair ;
illustrated by Claudia Wolf.
p. cm. — (Read-it! readers fairy tales)
Summary: An easy-to-read retelling of the classic tale of a girl whose stepmother, jealous
of Snow White's beauty, causes her to fall into a deep sleep.
ISBN 1-4048-0312-2 (Library Binding)
[1. Fairy tales. 2. Folklore—Germany.] I. Grimm, Jacob, 1785-1863. II. Grimm,
Wilhelm, 1786-1859. III. Wolf, Claudia, ill. IV. Snow White and the seven dwarfs.
English. V. Title. VI. Series.
PZ8.B5688Sn 2004
398.2—dc22   2003014037

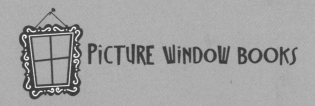

PICTURE WINDOW BOOKS

Snow White

A Retelling of the Grimms' Fairy Tale
By Eric Blair

Illustrated by Claudia Wolf

Content Adviser:
Kathy Baxter, M.A.
Former Coordinator of Children's Services
Anoka County (Minnesota) Library

Reading Advisers:
Adria F. Klein, Ph.D.
Professor Emeritus, California State University
San Bernardino, California

Susan Kesselring, M.A.
Literacy Educator
Rosemount-Apple Valley-Eagan (Minnesota) School District

Picture Window Books
Minneapolis, Minnesota

About the Brothers Grimm

To help a friend, brothers Jacob and Wilhelm
Grimm began collecting old stories told
in their home country of Germany. Events
in their lives would take the brothers away
from their project, but they never forgot
about it. Several years later, the Grimms
published their first books of fairy tales.
The stories they collected still are enjoyed
by children and adults today.

Once upon a time, there was a princess.
She had snow-white skin, blood-red lips,
rosy cheeks, and shiny black hair.
Her name was Snow White.

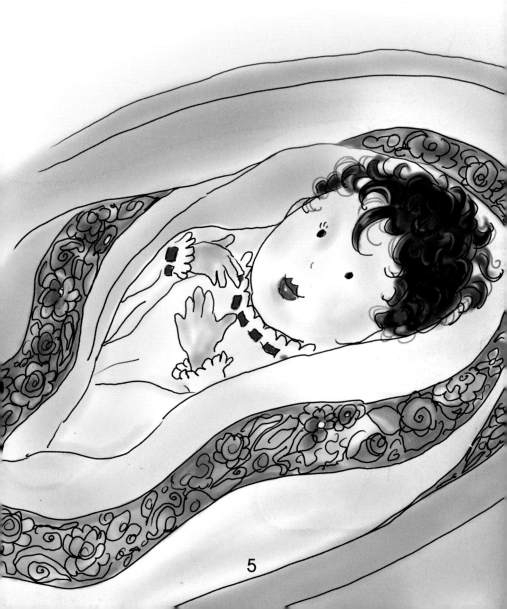

On the day Snow White was born,
her mother died. A year later, Snow White's
father took a new wife. This new queen
became Snow White's stepmother.
The queen was very proud of her own beauty.

The wicked queen had a magic mirror.
She would look into the mirror and ask,
"Mirror, mirror, on the wall, who's the fairest
of us all?"

7

The talking mirror would answer, "My lady queen is fairest of all." This made the evil queen happy.

Snow White grew more beautiful. One day, the mirror told the queen Snow White was the most beautiful person in the kingdom. This made the queen very jealous.

The queen told a hunter to take
Snow White into the forest and kill her.
Snow White begged for mercy. The hunter
felt sorry for her and let her go.

Snow White was alone and afraid. She wandered in the forest. At last Snow White found a cottage. She didn't know it, but it was the home of seven dwarfs.

Inside, Snow White found a tiny table
set for dinner. She was very hungry.
She took a little food from each plate.
Then Snow White lay down to sleep
in one of the seven tiny beds.

When the dwarfs came home from work,
they found the sleeping girl.

The next morning, Snow White woke up
and saw the dwarfs. She was afraid.
But the dwarfs were friendly.

Snow White told the dwarfs her story.
The dwarfs decided she could stay
with them if she kept the cottage clean.
Snow White gladly agreed.

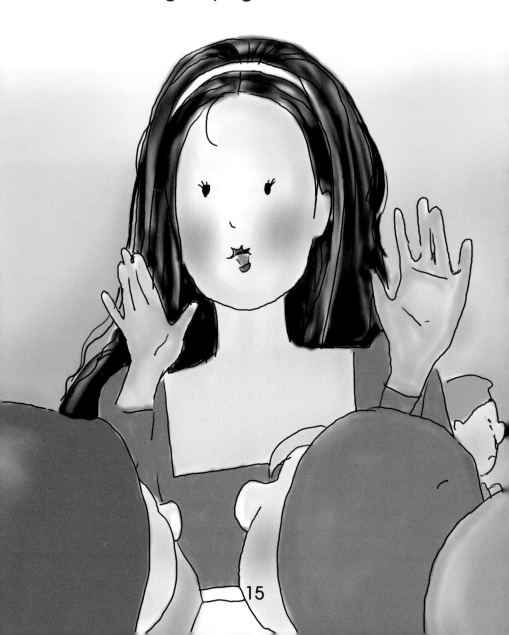

Each morning the dwarfs went to work.
They told Snow White to keep safe.
"Don't let anyone in the cottage,"
one dwarf warned.

16

The queen thought Snow White was dead.
One day the queen asked her magic mirror,
"Mirror, mirror, on the wall, who's the fairest of
us all?" The mirror said, "Snow White is fairest
of all. With the seven dwarfs she dwells."

The queen dressed up like an old woman.
She went to the dwarfs' cottage
and pretended to have things to sell.
"Good morning," Snow White said.
"What do you have to sell?"

The woman showed Snow White
a fancy comb. The comb was pretty,
but it was poisoned. The old woman
put the comb in Snow White's hair.
Snow White fell to the floor.

The dwarfs came home and found
Snow White on the floor. When they took
the comb from her hair, she woke up.

20

Snow White told the dwarfs about
the old woman. "That old woman was
really the wicked queen," one dwarf said.
"Don't open the door for anyone."

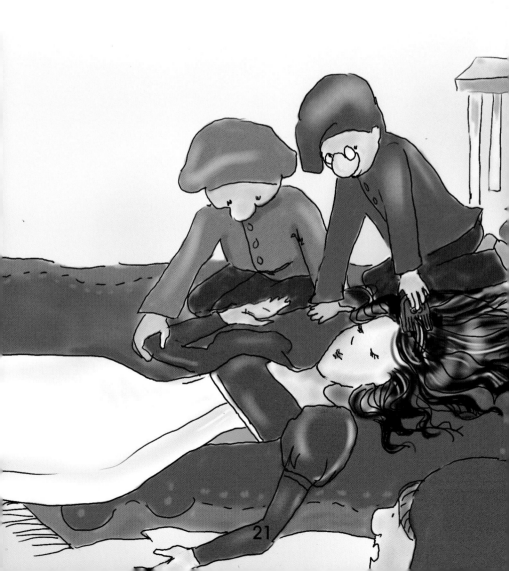

At the castle, the magic mirror told
the queen Snow White was still alive.
This time, the queen poisoned an apple
to kill Snow White.

The queen dressed as an old woman and went back to the cottage. She offered the apple to Snow White. Snow White wanted the apple, but she didn't trust the old woman.

But the queen was clever. She had put poison in only half of the apple. She took a bite from the half that wasn't poisoned to show Snow White the apple was safe.

Snow White took a bite of the other part of the apple and fell lifeless to the floor. When the dwarfs came home, they couldn't help Snow White.

The dwarfs did not have the heart to bury
Snow White. Instead, they built a coffin
of clear glass for her. They placed
the coffin on a hill in the forest.

But Snow White was not really dead.
For many years, she lay asleep
in the glass coffin. Her cheeks stayed rosy,
her lips red, her skin white, and her hair black.
A dwarf always stood guard.

One day, a prince came into the forest.
He saw the beautiful girl in the glass coffin.
"I can't live without her," he said.
The dwarfs let the prince have
Snow White because he loved her.

The prince's servants started carrying the coffin away. They stumbled, and the coffin was bumped. The piece of poisoned apple that had been stuck in Snow White's throat popped out. She opened her eyes and asked, "Where am I?"

"You are with me," said the prince.
"You are my true love. Please be my wife."
Snow White said she would marry the prince.
The prince and the dwarfs were very happy.

There was a fancy wedding. The wicked queen came. She recognized Snow White right away. The queen ran away and was never seen again. Snow White and the prince lived happily ever after.

31

Levels for *Read-it!* Readers

Read-it! Readers help children practice early reading skills
with brightly illustrated stories.

Red Level: Familiar topics with frequently used words and
repeating patterns.

Blue Level: New ideas with a larger vocabulary and a variety
of language structures.

Little Red Riding Hood, by Maggie Moore 1-4048-0064-6

The Three Little Pigs, by Maggie Moore 1-4048-0071-9

Yellow Level: Challenging ideas with an expanded vocabulary
and a wide variety of sentences.

Cinderella, by Barrie Wade 1-4048-0052-2

Goldilocks and the Three Bears, by Barrie Wade 1-4048-0057-3

Jack and the Beanstalk, by Maggie Moore 1-4048-0059-X

The Three Billy Goats Gruff, by Barrie Wade 1-4048-0070-0

Green Level: More complex ideas with an extended vocabulary
range and expanded language structures.

The Brave Little Tailor, by Eric Blair 1-4048-0315-7

The Bremen Town Musicians, by Eric Blair 1-4048-0310-6

The Emperor's New Clothes, by Susan Blackaby 1-4048-0224-X

The Fisherman and His Wife, by Eric Blair 1-4048-0317-3

The Frog Prince, by Eric Blair 1-4048-0313-0

Hansel and Gretel, by Eric Blair 1-4048-0316-5

The Little Mermaid, by Susan Blackaby 1-4048-0221-5

The Princess and the Pea, by Susan Blackaby 1-4048-0223-1

Rumpelstiltskin, by Eric Blair 1-4048-0311-4

The Shoemaker and His Elves, by Eric Blair 1-4048-0314-9

Snow White, by Eric Blair 1-4048-0312-2

The Steadfast Tin Soldier, by Susan Blackaby 1-4048-0226-6

Thumbelina, by Susan Blackaby 1-4048-0225-8

The Ugly Duckling, by Susan Blackaby 1-4048-0222-3